Hush, Little Baby

Adapted and illustrated by

Brian Pinkney

Greenwillow Books

An Imprint of HarperCollinsPublishers

Amistad

"Hush, Little Baby" is a Southern Appalachian lullaby that stems from the English tradition of nursery rhymes. Though many of us fell asleep in the arms of a loving parent who urged us to "hush, little baby," I wanted to put the song in an unexpected context. To that end, I created a visual narrative of a day in the life of an African American family in the early 1900s, in which Mama goes off for the day and Papa is left to tend to the young'uns.

I also drew from my own experience of having two young children, a boy and a girl. I tapped into the way I use playfulness as a means of consoling my kids. I have learned, though, that playfulness goes only so far. Nurturing can be expressed in many ways. There's make-believe, improvisation, whimsy. . . .

But even after the diamond ring turns brass and the spinning top will no longer twirl, the best way to comfort any child is through love.

—Brian Pinkney

Hush, Little Baby
Illustrations copyright © 2006 by Brian Pinkney
Arrangement copyright © 2006 by David Wolff
Amistad is an imprint of HarperCollins Publishers, Inc.
All rights reserved. Manufactured in China.
www.harperchildrens.com

Colored inks on clay board were used to prepare the full-color art.
The text type is 50-point Integrity JY Lining Medium 2.

Library of Congress Cataloging-in-Publication Data
Pinkney, J. Brian.
Hush, little baby / by Brian Pinkney.
  p. cm.
"Greenwillow Books."
Summary: An illustrated version of the traditional folk song
in which a father promises the world to his restless baby daughter.
ISBN-10: 0-06-055993-4 (trade bdg.) ISBN-13: 978-0-06-055993-9 (trade bdg.)
ISBN-10: 0-06-055994-2 (lib. bdg.) ISBN-13: 978-0-06-055994-6 (lib. bdg.)
1. Folk songs, English—Texts. [1. Lullabies. 2. Folk songs.] I. Title.
PZ8.3.P5586829Hus 2006 782.4215'82'0942—dc22 2005008216

First Edition 10 9 8 7 6 5 4 3 2 1

Greenwillow Books

For Virginia

Hush, little baby, don't say a word,

papa's gonna buy you

If that mockingbird

don't sing,

Papa's gonna

buy you a diamond ring.

If that diamond ring turns brass,

Papa's gonna buy you

a looking glass.

If that looking glass

should drop, Papa's gonna

buy you a spinning top.

If that spinning top won't twirl,

Papa's gonna bring

you a dog named Pearl.

If that dog named Pearl don't bark,

Papa's gonna bring you

a horse and cart.

If that horse and cart get stuck,

Papa's gonna bring you

Hush, little baby, don't you cry,

Mama's gonna sing you

a lullaby.

Hush, Little Baby

With a Caribbean feel ♩ = 96

Arranged by
David Wolff

Hush, lit-tle ba-by, don't say a word, Pa-pa's gon na buy you a mock - ing-bird.

If that mock-ing - bird don't sing, Pa-pa's gon-na buy you a di - a - mond ring.

1 Hush, little baby, don't say a word,
Papa's gonna buy you a mockingbird.
If that mockingbird don't sing,
Papa's gonna buy you a diamond ring.

2 If that diamond ring turns brass,
Papa's gonna buy you a looking glass.
If that looking glass should drop,
Papa's gonna buy you a spinning top.

3 If that spinning top won't twirl,
Papa's gonna bring you a dog named Pearl.
If that dog named Pearl don't bark,
Papa's gonna bring you a horse and cart.

4 If that horse and cart get stuck,
Papa's gonna bring you a fire truck!
Hush, little baby, don't you cry,
Mama's gonna sing you a lullaby.